Mystery
of the
Secret
Room

Mystery
of the
Secret
Room

BY JANELLE DILLER

ILLUSTRATIONS BY ADAM TURNER

Published by WorldTrek Publishing

Copyright © 2014 by Pack-n-Go Girls

Printed in the USA

Visit our website at www.packngogirls.com.

This is a work of fiction. Names, characters, places, and incidents either are the product of the author's imagination or are used fictitiously. The town of Kitzbühel, Austria, is real, and it's a wonderful place to visit. Any other resemblance to actual events, locales, organizations, or persons, living or dead, is entirely coincidental and beyond the intent of either the author or the publisher.

Illustrations by Adam Turner

ISBN 978-1-936376-03-2

Cataloging-in-Publication Data available from the Library of Congress.

In memory of my mother, who packed our suitcases and taught me to travel light.

Mystery of the Secret Room is the second book in the Pack-n-Go Girls Austria adventures. The first book, *Mystery of the Ballerina Ghost*, tells how Brooke and Eva first met. If you haven't read it yet, you won't want to miss it. Here's a bit about the book:

Nine-year-old Brooke Mason has lived all her life on a ranch in the Colorado Rockies. Now she's headed to Austria with her mom. Brooke can't wait! They even get to stay in Schloss Mueller, an ancient Austrian castle. Even better? There's a girl Brooke's age to play with. Eva, the girl who lives in Schloss Mueller, is thrilled to meet Brooke.

Unfortunately, the castle's ghost isn't quite so happy.

Contents

Meet the Characters

Brooke Mason is jazzed about visiting her Austrian friend, Eva.

Eva Mueller loves playing with her new American friend, Brooke.

Mrs. Mason is Brooke's mom. She loves art more than anything— except her family, of course.

Herr Mueller is Eva's grandfather. He's the master of the castle, Schloss Mueller.

Drew Bender works for Herr Mueller. But why has he come to Austria?

Frau Eder is the cook. She makes the best *Kaiserschmarrn* in Austria—maybe even the world!

The Secret Room
is full of unexplainable things.

And now, the mystery begins . . .

Chapter 1

Rainy Day Games

". . . acht, neun, zehn . . . Ich komme!"

Here I come.

Brooke could barely hear Eva's voice as it drifted up the stairs into the attic. She should be tucked away in a hiding place by now. But she was still frantically looking for a good spot. She carefully moved some boxes to crouch behind. A spider darted across the new empty space. She jumped back and whispered, "Yikes!"

Her heart pounded. Thump, thump, thump.

Did Eva hear her jump?

She held her breath and listened for her friend's footsteps on the stairs.

The only sound was the rain tap, tap, tapping on the window. A door screeched opened on the floor below and Eva called in a singsongy voice. *"Wo bist du?"* Where are you? Brooke was happy her German was getting better. Eva had been teaching her phrases, which was a good thing. If she was going to spend time with her Austrian friend, she should be able to speak a little German.

It sounded like Eva had moved away from the attic door. That gave her a few more minutes to hide. But where?

The cluttered room had a gazillion dark corners and even more shadows. White sheets covered furniture shapes. They seemed to glow in the grey afternoon light. If Brooke were cross-my-heart-

hope-to-die honest, it was a little too spooky. Even though Eva's ballerina ghost had turned out to be a trick Eva played, Brooke still remembered how scary it was to see the "ghost" in the attic window. After all, if a ghost did live in Schloss Mueller, this dusty old space would be the perfect place for it to hang out.

Maybe she shouldn't have come up here to hide.

Too late now. She should have thought about this earlier. But she and Eva had hidden in all the good places already. The attic seemed like such a smart idea when Brooke was on the floor below.

Where the windows were big.

And the noises were friendly.

And there weren't so many creepy, eepy shadows.

Brooke sighed. She opened the door of a tall wooden cabinet. Clothes. She should have guessed it was some kind of closet. Then it struck her. It was a wardrobe like in *The Lion, the Witch, and the Wardrobe*. She sniffed. The sharp, woody scent reminded her of a closet in her grandma's house where she kept her winter sweaters.

She closed the door and glanced around the room again. Surely, somewhere in this room was a good—no, a great—hiding place.

"*Wo bist du?*"

Eva's voice sounded like she was at the foot of the attic stairs. What if she noticed the door was slightly open?

The attic door creaked.

Too late.

"*Ich weiß, dass du hier oben bist.*" I know you're up here.

Brooke only had three seconds. She yanked open the wardrobe door again and scrambled in. Better in here, she thought, than where the spiders live. Ever so quietly, she pulled the door shut behind her and tucked into a corner. A silky fur coat draped down over her and a man's hat tumbled into her lap.

Eva's footsteps crept up the attic stairs. "Brooke?" Her voice shook a little. "Are you here?"

Brooke giggled inside. This might be fun after all. Eva would never find her snuggled into this clothes closet. She felt safe from spiders and ghosts for the moment. Her back rested firmly against the side of the closet. She might even have the courage to say BOO if Eva opened the door.

She giggled again inside.

She could hear Eva poking around the room. Boxes scraped on the floor. Once she heard Eva shriek, "Ack!"

"Ahhh," Brooke thought. "She found *Herr* Spider." She scooted around carefully to get more comfortable. Several boards were missing along the back of the wardrobe. When she leaned back again between the missing boards, her head bumped something. A knob of some kind.

Quietly, she felt for it in the dark. It was smooth and round and about the size of a golf ball. It turned easily, just like a small doorknob.

How odd, Brooke thought. Doorknobs are for the outside of closets, not the inside. Cautiously, she pulled on the knob. A door—really it was just half of a door—opened. Brooke had an uneasy flash. Wasn't this how Lucy ended up in Narnia?

Oddly enough, it wasn't dark. Brooke could see a tiny bit of light, like there was a window far beyond the door. Well, she thought, at least it's not snowing in there. It can't be Narnia. She immediately felt silly for such a thought.

And maybe a little disappointed.

The clothes in the wardrobe pressed against the door, but she still tugged it open a tiny bit further. It took a minute for her eyes to adjust to the dim light. Was it just a small, empty room? It had to be more, though. The light had to come from somewhere. Why would there be an old wardrobe in front of a door to another room?

What a PERFECT hiding spot, Brooke thought, except I'm too chicken to explore it.

"Brooke?" A floorboard squeaked on the far side of the room. "I see footprints in the dust. I know you're up here. I'm not giving up!" The words sounded brave.

I can be brave, too, thought Brooke. She sighed inside because even as she thought it, she doubted it.

"Come out now!" Eva said. Brooke could hear her stomp her foot. "I know you're more scared of the dark than I am!"

Brooke didn't care that it was true. How dare she say that! She'd show her. She shoved the little door open far enough to squeeze through. She slipped into the space and softly closed the door behind her.

Again, her heart thump, thump, thumped.

Slowly, her eyes got used to the low light. She seemed to be in a long and very narrow room, no wider than a couch. Above her, the low ceiling slanted toward what must be an outside wall. She thought she could almost stand up straight on the short side of the wall, but she couldn't touch the ceiling on the high side. Up ahead, she could see light coming in from about halfway down the room.

Dusty sheets covered shapes of all sizes, just like it was in the rest of the attic. They lined the wall like ghostly soldiers. Brooke felt dizzy from her heart pounding so hard. But she crept through the narrow room toward the light. Where was it coming from? She bumped against a sheet-covered box. It tumbled to the floor, clanking like a bunch of silverware.

On the other side of the wardrobe, Eva called to her. "Brooke? I heard that. Where are you? You sound like you're in the wall." Her voice didn't sound so brave anymore.

Brooke barely heard her, though. Only a few more steps.

Carefully, she felt her way through the dim hallway until she reached where the light came from. When she turned the corner, she couldn't believe her eyes. A shiver ran from the top of her head to the tip of her toes.

"Oh my," she said, barely breathing.

"Brooke! Are you okay? Where are you?"

"Eva!" she shouted back to her friend. "You won't believe what I just discovered!"

Chapter Two

The Discovery

"Brooke! Where are you?" Eva called out.

"I'm in here. Behind the wardrobe." She stumbled through the dim light until she got back to the little half door. She turned the knob, but the door seemed stuck. Her stomach turned upside down. What if she were trapped? "Eva!" She pounded on the small door. "Eva, can you hear me?"

"I can hear you, but I can't find you."

Eva's voice was just on the other side of the door.

"Are you in the wardrobe?" Brooke asked.

"Yes. Where are you? It sounds like you're behind the wardrobe in the wall."

"That's exactly where I am. Can you find the doorknob on the back of the wardrobe? It's where the fur coat is hanging."

Brooke could hear Eva fumbling on the other side. "Can you find it? It's lower than you would expect it to be."

"Got it," Eva said at last.

"Good. Now pull hard."

Brooke heard a dull thump. Suddenly, the door burst open, and Eva poked her head into the small hallway.

"Was? Was ist das?" German words flew from Eva's mouth.

"Whoa!" Brooke laughed. "I can't understand a

word you're saying. Isn't this crazy?" She pulled on her friend's arm. "You have to see this. You're not going to believe it."

The two girls felt their way along the hall like Brooke had only a few minutes earlier. "Close your eyes, Eva."

"I already can't see," she said. She sounded annoyed.

"Just do it. I want you to be completely surprised."

Eva sighed, but she squeezed her eyes shut. Brooke gently led her friend around the corner. "Now open them."

Eva gasped. Finally, she whispered, "This is amazing."

In front of the girls lay a small room no bigger than a large closet. Dust and cobwebs crisscrossed the room. Except for that, it looked like someone had been expecting them. A red wooden table with two matching chairs stood to one side. Long, long ago, someone had set it for a fancy tea party. A lace tablecloth with cross-stitched red hearts covered the tabletop like a diamond. In the middle of the table, a pink heart-shaped teapot with two tiny pink cups and saucers on each side looked ready for guests. A tin of butter cookies lay next to the teapot. Best of all, a porcelain doll sat in a doll highchair next to the table. She wore a long, gauzy dress like a baby might wear to its christening. Maybe it had been white

The Discovery

once. Now, like everything else, it was dingy with a coat of dust. The doll stared at the two girls. Her red lips pouted slightly, as though she were mad the girls were late.

A child-sized cabinet with four drawers stood on the other wall. It, too, had been painted red with white hearts. At the narrow end of the room, a window, cloudy with age, let in the gray afternoon light. A million years ago the lacy curtain on it had been white, but no more.

"It's . . . it's wonderful," Eva said when she finally breathed again.

"So you didn't know this room was here?"

"No. It's unbelievable, isn't it?"

"How is it possible that you didn't know about it?" Brooke asked. She knew every single corner and cabinet in her own house.

Eva shrugged her shoulders. "The castle is big. Lots of rooms are closed because we don't use them. But this . . . this . . ." Her voice dropped to a whisper. For the first time since Brooke had met her, Eva couldn't think of a single thing to say. In English or in German.

"Who could have left this?" Brooke asked. "And why would they leave the doll here?"

"I don't know. But it's like they were expecting us." Eva shuddered and lowered her voice. "You don't think there's a *real* ghost do you?" She didn't sound brave at all now.

"Eva! Don't try to scare me." Brooke looked behind her. What if someone—or something—appeared?

"I'm not. Honest!" Her voice dropped to a whisper. "But this is just really, really, really creepy. Don't you think?"

"Maybe. So who could it have been?"

"I don't know. But maybe she was a princess whose mother died in a tragic accident. Then her father married a mean old witch so—"

"So," Brooke said, finishing Eva's sentence, "the princess brought her favorite doll and hid out in this attic room—"

"And then a handsome prince found her and saved her."

The girls laughed at their goofy story.

"Except why would she leave her doll?" Eva asked.

The girls stopped laughing. The question gave Brooke goosebumps. Why would someone just leave everything like they would be back in a minute? It was too spooky.

Eva picked up the doll and shook the dust from her dress. "Isn't she beautiful?" She held her like a baby and the doll's eyelids closed shut, making a quiet clicking sound. She blew the dust off of her face.

"I wonder if there are any more clothes for

her," Brooke said. She opened up a drawer in the dresser. "Look at this, Eva."

"A fancy scarf. Like you'd wear skiing."

"And look at this!" Brooke held up a chain with a nearly black heart-shaped locket and some kind of fancy design on the cover. "Who would give someone a black locket?"

"Not a prince, that's for sure!"

Brooke fiddled with the catch on the side of the locket. Finally, the cover popped open. In one half of the locket lay a picture of a young girl. She might have been the age of Brooke and Eva. Her curly hair had a fluffy bow on the side. The girl looked very serious.

On the other side was a picture of a woman with short, wavy hair. She wore a light blouse and dark jacket. Her head tilted slightly and she had a small smile, as though she knew a secret.

"She's beautiful," Eva said.

"And mysterious looking."

"It must be the girl and her mother, don't you think?"

Brooke scrunched up her nose. "Maybe. But why would she leave the doll and a locket with her mother's picture in it."

"Maybe she was kidnapped."

Brooke shivered. "Or maybe she suddenly died of some terrible disease."

"And she didn't have the strength to climb the steps one last time to get the locket and doll before she died."

The Discovery

"How awful!" Brooke felt like she could cry just thinking about it.

Eva opened another drawer. "Nothing but old books."

Brooke picked up one and started paging through it. "Look at these silly illustrations." The pages had a few pictures, but they were only black silhouettes of people and things.

Eva snorted. "Who'd want to read a book with those pictures?"

Brooke turned to the inside cover. "What's this say? The letters have too many swirls for me to read."

Eva traced the letters with her fingers. "Huh?" She scrunched up her nose and gave Brooke an odd look. "It says 'Eva.'"

"Eva? What—"

"Eva. Eva Mueller."

Goosebumps marched down Brooke's arms.

"But that's you. How can your name be in this book? Was there another Eva Mueller?"

"I don't know. I don't think so."

Brooke picked up the locket again and ran her fingertips over the cover. "Eva, feel this. What letter do you think is on this?"

Eva studied the cover and felt the pattern. "It's an *E*."

"*E* for Eva," Brooke whispered. "For *you*."

"This is too creepy!"

The girls looked at each other and almost in unison said, "Let's get out of here!"

Chapter Three

The Name in the Book

"Grossvater! Grossvater!"

"Mom! Mom!"

The girls' voices tangled together as they raced down the stairs.

Herr Mueller, Eva's grandfather, called out to them. "I'm in the library, girls. Brooke, your mother went into the village for some supplies." Herr Mueller had hired Mrs. Mason, Brooke's mom, to organize his large collection of American paintings.

This was the second time in a single summer that Mrs. Mason and Brooke had come to Schloss Mueller in Kitzbühel, Austria.

The girls flew through the door together and into the cozy, book-filled room.

Eva ran to her grandfather. "You're not going to believe what we found!"

"Not another ghost, I hope," Herr Mueller said. His face still looked stern and a little scary to Brooke, but she knew on the inside he was a kind man. "You can tell me in a minute. First, I want to introduce you to Drew Bender." He motioned to a young man standing by the fireplace. Brooke hadn't noticed him until that moment. He looked a little older than Brooke's oldest brother. She guessed he was almost old enough to go to college. "He's going to be working here the rest of the summer and into the fall. He'll help with the horses and the gardens."

"How do you do, Drew. I'm Brooke," Brooke

said and shook his hand. She said it as politely as she could even though she was itching on the inside to tell Herr Mueller about the secret room.

"How do you do, Mr. Bender. My name is *Fräulein* Eva Mueller." She shook Drew's hand, too, but she talked fast, like she was impatient.

The young man smiled a half smile. "I can tell which girl is the American and which one is the Austrian."

Herr Mueller raised a tangled eyebrow. "We're

doing our best to teach Brooke how to behave like an Austrian. But I'm afraid once an American, always an American." He winked at Brooke.

Brooke straightened up and solemnly put her hand out again to shake Drew's hand. *"Grüß Gott, Herr Bender. Ich bin Brooke Mason und freue mich, sie kennenzulernen."*

"Ahh," Herr Mueller said and patted Brooke's shoulder. "That's more like it."

"Grüß Gott, Fraulein. Ich freue mich, dich kennenzulernen," the young man responded in flawless German. He even used the Austrian greeting *Grüß Gott* correctly. "But please call me Drew." He laughed and added, "All of you." He nodded in Herr Mueller's direction.

"I'll never get used to how informal you Americans are." He shook his head. "Mr. Bender— Drew is from America also. The state of Wyoming, isn't that right?" He looked at Drew, who nodded.

"Eva, that's close to Colorado, where Brooke lives."

"We're almost neighbors," Drew said. He smiled a broad, cheerful smile. Brooke liked his sun-browned skin and blue eyes. He was tall, lean, and muscular.

"Almost," Herr Mueller said and patted Drew's back. "Now that you've met the girls, I'll take you to meet our housekeeper, Frau Eder. She'll take you to your room and show you around."

"Grandfather," Eva said softly and tugged at the old man's arm. "We want to tell you what we found in the attic."

"Oh, of course. I almost forgot your new ghost." Herr Mueller winked at Drew.

"It's not a ghost," Eva said impatiently. "It's better than that."

"What could be better than a ghost, *Liebling*?" He laughed but not in a mean way.

"We found a secret room in the attic—"

Eva began.

"A secret room?" Herr Mueller said. He stiffened slightly. "What do you mean?"

"We found a door in an old wardrobe and it took us to a secret room," Eva said again.

"It had a table and chairs and a beautiful doll," Brooke added.

"And this book with my name in it!" Eva held out the dusty book.

Herr Mueller took it from Eva's hand. He opened the cover and stared at the fancy script.

"Who else is named Eva Mueller? I thought I was the only one."

"Where did you say you found this?" he asked. His voice sounded tight, almost mean.

"We just told you, Grandfather. In the attic. Brooke and I found a secret room—"

Herr Mueller snapped the book shut. "You shouldn't be playing up there. It's not safe."

The Name in the Book

"But Grandfather—"

"Du hast mich schon richtig verstanden." You heard me.

"It's the coolest place," Brooke jumped in. Surely he didn't understand. "It's like a girl our age played there. We also found a lock—" Brooke felt Eva's elbow poke her.

"What did you find?" Herr Mueller asked.

"Uh . . . well . . . a lot. We found a lot of stuff up there," Eva said as though she were finishing Brooke's sentence.

The old man studied the two girls but didn't say anything. His mouth grew into a tight, straight line.

"Why can't we play up there?"

Finally, he took a slow, deep breath. *"Weil ich es sage."* Because I said so. It meant the same thing in every language. The discussion is closed. Brooke clearly understood the words. What she couldn't figure out was why Herr Mueller sounded so angry.

Even more puzzling was the look on Drew's face. The smile and twinkle in his eyes were gone. His eyes grew narrow and his jaw looked tense. This wasn't the happy boy she'd just met.

How could an old book make both of them so upset?

Chapter Four

The Decision

"I don't get it," Eva said. "He never cared before if we played in the attic. Why now?"

The girls were stretched out across Eva's fluffy lavender bed. They stared out the window and watched the raindrops make little rivers down the window. Outside, everything looked as green as a jungle. Inside, though, it was gloomy.

"Who can ever figure out grown-ups?" Brooke said.

"I'll bet if we were in Colorado, your mom

would let us play in the attic."

"Maybe." Brooke shook her head. "I don't know."

"Why did he get so mad?"

"I don't know. It's weird. Did you see that new guy's reaction?"

"Drew? What do you mean?"

"He looked mad too. Why would he care?"

Eva shrugged her shoulders. "Maybe he just realized he traveled halfway around the world to shovel horse manure."

Brooke snorted. "Oh, yeah. He could have stayed at home and done the same thing. Trust me, there's plenty of horse manure in Wyoming to shovel." The more she thought about it, the funnier it sounded.

Eva started giggling. "What do you think he did? Fly to Austria and then start knocking on doors and asking if people wanted any manure shoveled?"

The Decision

Brooke jumped to her feet and pretended to knock on a door. "*Grüß Gott, mein Herr. Haben Sie any—*" she looked at her friend for help. "How do you say 'horse manure' in German?"

"*Pferdeäpfel.*"

"Of course." She slapped her forehead. She pretended to knock again. "Herr Mueller, do you have any *Pferdeäpfel* to shovel?"

"Your mom will be so proud of how much German you learned today!"

"And I'm going to practice at dinner tonight."

They were both laughing so hard by now they could hardly breathe.

"There's just one thing," Eva said when she could finally stop laughing.

"What's that?"

"Why *would* someone travel halfway around the world to shovel horse manure? And then why would he get mad about an old book we found in an attic."

"Something's weird here."

"It's not what it looks like."

"No, it's not."

The two girls sat silent for a while. They thought about how odd everything was.

"So what do you think we should do?" Brooke finally asked.

"I think we should go clean up our new playroom," Eva said. She had a sly smile on her face.

"But won't your grandfather

get mad if we go back to the attic?"

"Maybe," Eva said. She paused a minute and looked at Brooke. "Maybe not."

"I don't know, Eva. We could get in big trouble."

"Oh, come on. What's the worst that could happen?"

"My mom wouldn't let me come back to Austria. That's the worst thing that could happen."

"Well, besides that."

"What do you mean? That would be pretty awful."

"Yeah, but it's not going to happen."

Brooke had to agree. Both her mom and Herr Mueller liked that the girls had—as they called it—an "international friendship."

"I think my grandfather would be mad, but he wouldn't do anything. Really."

"Then what are you saying?"

"I'm saying," Eva stood up and put her hands on her hips. "We should go clean up that room. Our *secret* room."

Chapter Five

The Black Locket

The girls gathered up a broom, some old rags, and a bucket of water. They wiped and washed and swept and shined everything that could be wiped, washed, swept, and shined.

Before long, the room looked and smelled like a happy place to play.

"Now," Eva said. "We have just one more thing to do."

"What's that?"

"Clean up this locket."

"What do you mean? It's just a black locket."

"I don't think so. The more I think about it, the more it reminds me of our silverware that Frau Eder polishes. It can get almost black. Then she rubs this special stuff on it. It gets all shiny and silvery again."

"What does she use?"

Eva shrugged her shoulders. "Stuff." She fingered the locket. "I don't know, but we'll figure it out."

The girls found Frau Eder in the kitchen doing what she was always doing: cooking. Brooke couldn't be sure, but it looked like she was mixing the batter for *Kaiserschmarrn*, the sweet Austrian pancake.

"Ummmm, Frau Eder," Brooke said as she peeked in the mixing bowl. "Are you making my most favorite dessert?"

The Black Locket

"Ja, ja," Frau Eder said as she separated the egg whites from the egg yolks. "You like *Kaiserschmarrn*, Fraulein Brooke?"

"I love, love, love it so much I wish I could marry it."

Frau Eder looked confused. "My English *ist* not so *gut*."

Eva translated. "She loves it Frau Eder. And we love you for making it." She threw her arms around the woman. Brooke joined her friend and hugged Frau Eder too. The woman laughed happily but shooed them away.

"I should make *Kaiserschmarrn* all days," she said. She pulled up a couple of kitchen stools and told the girls to sit and watch so they could learn to make it.

Brooke was perfectly happy watching and, she hoped, eating. But Eva remembered why they had come down to the kitchen.

"Frau Eder?"

"Ja, Liebling?"

"I was telling Brooke about how we have to polish our silverware with special stuff to make it shiny."

"Ja?"

"Can I show her?" Eva asked.

"You want to show her how we make the silver shiny?"

Both girls nodded. They must have looked too excited. Frau Eder gave Eva a look like Brooke's mom did sometimes. Brooke didn't think she believed them.

"The polish and cloth are in there." She pointed with her head to a cabinet. "You know where the silver is."

Eva gathered the things together and put them on the table. "Now what?"

"Now you put a little polish on the cloth and

rub the silver. Rub, rub, rub."

Brooke took a spoon that looked more grey than silver. She dipped the cloth into the creamy paste and spread it on the spoon. As she rubbed, the cloth turned black.

"Now with a clean cloth, you rub it again."

Brooke took a clean corner of the rag and rubbed it again. It shone like a mirror. "Wow! That's cool." She sincerely meant it. "Can I do another one?"

"*Ja*, of course." Frau Eder watched her for a minute. She shook her head and then went back to her batter.

Brooke polished several more spoons. This was actually fun. Meanwhile, Eva helped herself to some polish, too. She slipped the locket out of her pocket and rubbed the paste on it. Just as she had thought, the black started to disappear. She repeated the process three more times.

Eva kicked Brooke under the table. Brooke looked up and Eva showed her the locket, which was now bright and shiny. The *E* still had a little of the black tarnish around it.

"It's beautiful!" Brooke said out loud without thinking about where they were.

"What?" Frau Eder said and turned just in time to see the locket disappear into Eva's pocket.

"Eva? What is going on?"

"Nothing, Frau Eder. Really."

The Black Locket

Frau Eder gave her another mom look and said something in German that Brooke didn't understand.

Eva sighed. But she pulled the locket from her pocket.

Frau Eder opened the locket. She gave a small gasp and snapped the locket shut. "Where you get this?"

"Do you know who she is?" Eva asked without answering Frau Eder's question.

"Eva. I ask you a question. Where you get this?"

Eva shifted in her seat. She wouldn't look Frau Eder in the eye.

"Brooke?"

Brooke had always been a lousy liar. Her mom said that was a good thing. But Brooke wasn't so sure. The skill surely would be handy right now. Finally, she said, "We found it in our secret room."

Eva immediately scrunched up her nose at her. It didn't take a detective for Brooke to know Eva was mad at her.

"Secret?" Frau Eder asked.

"Geheimnis." Eva translated the word into German.

"I understand the word. I don't understand the meaning."

"We found a little door in the attic. It led to a tiny room with a table and chairs and a beautiful doll. We found the locket there."

Brooke watched Frau Eder. She tried to figure out if she was angry like Herr Mueller and Drew had been. But she looked more sad than mad. "I see," she said. "What else did you find?"

"Are you going to keep the locket?" Eva asked her. Again, she asked a question instead of answering one.

"No. It's not mine to keep." She set the locket

on the table. "What else you find?"

"We found some books," Brooke said.

Eva looked up. "Did you know there was another little girl named Eva Mueller?"

"Where you hear about this girl?"

"One of the books had her name on it," Eva said. "No one told me there was another Eva Mueller. Who was she?"

Frau Eder wiped her hands on her apron. She leaned against the counter and looked out the window. The rain had finally stopped, but the sun stayed hidden. "Is a sad story."

"Why is it sad? Did she die? Did she run away?" The questions tumbled out of Eva and Brooke.

Frau Eder shook her head. "I don't know."

"What do you mean you don't know?"

"I don't know." She went back to the batter. "Is before my time here at Schloss Mueller."

"But you know about her."

"*Ja*, some things."

"Then tell us about her. Please."

"Pretty please?" Brooke said.

Frau Eder looked puzzled. "Pretty please? I don't know this meaning."

"It's like the *Kaiserschmarrn* of please," Eva told her.

Frau Eder smiled. "Ah, is sweet and good."

"Yup," Brooke said.

Frau Eder shook her head. "Sorry. Is not my story to tell you."

"What do you mean? If you know it, why can't you tell us?"

"Is a story for your grandfather to tell you."

"But who was she?"

"Sorry, girls." She shook her head again. "Does your grandfather know about the secret room?"

Both girls nodded.

"And the book with the name in it?"

They nodded again.

"Then he knows he has to tell you the story."

Chapter Six

The Secret

Eva was pouting. Brooke knew the look. She'd pouted lots of times herself. But when her best friend did it, it annoyed her.

Frau Eder had made them go outside to play because it was finally sunny. So they were sitting on the back patio by the rose garden. Beyond the flowers, the mountain curved gently upwards in a haze of fresh green pasture. A small herd of cows grazed on the lush grass. Each animal had a bell that clanged a different tone. The air smelled clean and sharp like it does after a good rain. Any other time, the day would have been perfect. Absolutely perfect.

But today, neither girl noticed. They both wanted to play in the secret room, not outside on this gorgeous day.

Eva pulled the locket from her pocket. She rubbed it on her jeans even though it already gleamed.

"It must have been very expensive," Brooke said.

Eva nodded. "It's such a fancy design." She opened the locket and sighed. "I just wish we knew the secret. Who is Eva Mueller? And what happened to her?"

"It sounds like quite the mystery," a man's voice said.

The girls looked up to see Drew kneeling in the

middle of the roses. He wore gardening gloves and held clippers. It spooked Brooke to see him there. How long had he been listening?

"It is a mystery," Eva said. Now it was Brooke's turn to gently poke her friend with her elbow. He looked happy again, like he did when they first met him. But that didn't mean they could trust him.

Drew stood up and brushed his knees off. He stepped on to the patio and pointed to the locket. "Say, is that something else you found in your secret room?"

Eva closed the locket and put it back in her pocket. She nodded though.

"Can I see it? It sure looks shiny."

The girls looked at each other. It seemed rude not to show him. But Brooke could tell that Eva didn't want to share the locket any more than she did.

The boy laughed in a friendly way. "I promise

The Secret

I'll be careful." He knelt in front of them and held out his hand.

Reluctantly, Eva took out the locket and put it in his palm.

He didn't open it right away, though. Instead, with his finger, he traced the *E* on the cover.

Brooke watched his face. Like this morning, his eyes narrowed and his jaw grew tight. A small smile stayed on his face. Her stomach flopped upside down. What was he thinking? Was he planning to steal the locket?

"It's beautiful, isn't it?" He turned the locket over and studied the design. "It looks like *Edelweiss*. Do you know about this flower, Brooke?"

She shook her head.

"I'll bet Eva does."

His face relaxed a little. He said it in such a kind voice that Eva smiled and said, "It's a rare mountain flower that's small and white. It's special if you see one."

The Secret

Drew nodded. "I'll bet someone had this specially made for a special little girl. *Edelweiss* and Eva both start with the letter *E*. I'm sure that was no accident." He carefully opened the locket. Again, Brooke watched his face. His smile grew a little and his eyes softened.

"Who do you think they are?" he asked.

"We don't know for sure. But we think the girl must be Eva and the lady is her mother."

"You never know," he said and closed the locket.

Brooke thought it was an odd response. Shouldn't he have said, "That's what I would think," or something like that? It only made sense that it would be a mother and a daughter.

"So where is this secret room?"

This time, neither girl had to poke the other one. It didn't seem quite right that he should ask about the room.

"It's up there," Eva finally said. She nodded toward the attic. But it was so casual that she could have meant anywhere.

"Well, it would be fun to see it. You'll have to show me sometime." He smiled again. Brooke didn't like the smile.

"We can't. Grandfather said we can't play there anymore."

"Well, you wouldn't want to disobey your grandfather." He paused and looked up at the attic. "At least not a second time."

"What do you mean?" Both girls said almost in unison. As soon as they said it, Brooke cringed. It wouldn't take a rocket scientist to hear the guilt in *that* question.

"I mean, you had to go back to your secret room to get the locket after your grandfather told you not to."

"How do you know we didn't already have it?"

Eva said.

"Because that's what you would have showed him this morning instead of the book."

He was right, and Brooke knew it.

"But I tell you what. It'll be our little secret that you disobeyed him." He handed the locket back to Eva and winked.

He headed off toward the roses, then stopped and turned. "I can't wait for you to show me that room."

Chapter Seven

The Hiding Place

"The nerve of him!" Brooke was almost spitting she was so mad. She threw herself on Eva's bed.

"He's such a . . . a . . ."

"Snake!"

"Yeah. That's the word. At least I think it's the word," Eva said. She put her hands on her hips and snorted. "He's not going to tell on us if he gets to see the secret room? How dare he threaten us?"

"The nerve of him!" Brooke said again. "I don't

like him."

"I don't trust him."

"You know what I think, Eva?"

"That he's going to try to steal the locket?"

"Maybe. He was too curious about the secret room and the locket."

"Then we have to hide it."

"That should be easy enough. There have to be a gazillion places to hide something as small as a locket."

The two girls sat on the bed, legs crossed, chins in their hands.

"What about hiding it somewhere in my bedroom?"

"Too obvious. That's the first place he'd look."

"What about the kitchen?"

Brooke shook her head. "Frau Eder's in there too much. And what if she found it and showed it to him? You know he'll be getting all friendly with her because of all that good cooking."

"We could hide it in the library."

"Maybe. But my mom and your grandfather spend too much time in there."

The girls both sighed.

"Well, maybe there aren't a gazillion places to hide it."

"You know," Brooke finally said. "The safest place is in the secret room. He doesn't even know where the room is."

Eva perked up. "You're right. Even if he thinks that's where we hid it, he'd have to figure out where the room is."

"He'll never even find the door!"

"Unless we let him play hide and seek with us." Eva laughed at her good joke.

"Well, I'm never playing hide and seek with that creepy guy."

The girls slipped out into the hallway. They

could hear Herr Mueller's and Mrs. Mason's voices coming from the library. Eva quietly opened the attic door and the girls crept up the steps.

Eva crawled into the wardrobe first and opened the half door. Brooke followed her friend through the soft fur coats and into the half-lighted hallway.

"Now where would be a good place?" Brooke said.

"Not the drawers. That's the first place someone would look."

"How about the cookie tin? Or the teapot?"

Eva shook her head. "Too easy."

They studied the room. Unfortunately, there just weren't many places to hide something.

"I've got it!" Brooke snapped her fingers. She took the locket from Eva and draped it over the doll's head. She tucked the locket and chain under the doll's dress. She smiled. "You can't even see a trace of it."

"Perfect!"

"Now let's get out of here before your grandfather comes to get us for dinner."

Chapter Eight

No Clues

"What a wonderful idea to eat on the patio tonight," Mrs. Mason said.

"It was Frau Eder's idea," said Herr Mueller. "She said we shouldn't waste such a beautiful evening."

"I couldn't agree more."

Off in the distance, a couple of cows mooed. Their cowbells clanged softly. On the other side of the hedges, Brooke heard the sound of digging.

Apparently, Eva didn't. Maybe she figured that the beautiful evening was the perfect time to bring up a touchy subject. Or maybe she was crazy. Brooke wasn't sure.

"Grandfather, when will you tell me about the other Eva Mueller?"

Brooke kicked her under the table. When Eva looked, Brooke tilted her head toward the digging. But the digging had stopped. Brooke knew why.

Herr Mueller sighed. "*Liebling*, it's a sad story. You're too young to understand."

Mrs. Mason looked at Brooke. She had a puzzled expression.

"I am not too young." If Eva had been standing, Brooke was sure she would have stomped her foot. "Did you know there was a secret room in the attic?"

"I'd forgotten about that room a long time ago." His shoulders drooped.

"So you knew there was a hidden room and you didn't tell me?" Eva sounded annoyed, like she couldn't believe he'd never told her.

"Not exactly. I knew there was a hidden room somewhere up there, but I never knew where it was."

"What do you mean? How could you know there was a secret room but you didn't know where

it was? You've lived here all your life."

He sighed again. "*Liebling*, some day, I'll tell you the story, but it's a story from long, long ago. From before you were born—before I was born. It will make you cry, and I don't want you to cry."

"I *won't cry*!" Now she sounded a little mad. "Just tell me."

Herr Mueller shook his head. He said something to Eva in German. It sounded to Brooke like he was trying to tell her not to ask one more time, especially not in front of their guests. But she couldn't be sure. He smiled then and spoke in English again. "I have a special surprise for all of you. I have tickets to the ballet in Salzburg for tomorrow night. Let's leave early and enjoy the city. It's a beautiful place to spend the day!"

They should have been very excited. Eva loved ballet and Brooke had never spent time in Salzburg. But neither girl was happy with how this conversation ended.

Brooke wondered what Drew was thinking since the digging had started again.

Chapter Nine

Salzburg!

Herr Mueller was right about one thing: Salzburg was a beautiful city. Brooke loved Kitzbühel, the little village near Schloss Mueller. But it could hardly compare to Salzburg.

The small city sat on the Salzach River, which curved gracefully along the old part of town where cars weren't allowed. The cobblestone streets and stone arches made Brooke wish she had lived hundreds of years earlier. She would have been glad to walk past the shops and cafes, a basket of bread and fresh flowers on her arm.

Street vendors grilled bratwurst—a kind of sausage—and smothered it in mustard and sauerkraut, which Brooke knew was a kind of spicy pickled cabbage. The yummy smell made her crazy. Several street corners had stands with giant warm pretzels or gingerbread hearts. In the distance, a band with accordions and trumpets played. Right then and there, Brooke decided someday she would

live in Austria, not just visit it.

They toured the house that Wolfgang Amadeus Mozart lived in. Brooke could hardly breathe just thinking that she walked on the *very same floor* as Mozart had once walked. Afterwards, they bought Mozart Chocolates, which only had the name in common with her favorite composer. But, as they all agreed, you can never have too many chocolates.

For the moment, she forgot about the mystery of the other Eva Mueller. And the locket. And Drew.

Well almost.

"What do you think he's doing right now?" Eva whispered to her late in the morning.

"Just what you think. He's looking for the secret room. And he has a whole day to do it." As much fun as Brooke was having, she felt a little grim.

"Girls, come along. We don't want to miss the

Salzburg!

Sound of Music tour," Mrs. Mason said.

"The what?" Eva asked.

"The *Sound of Music* tour." Brooke rolled her eyes. "It's my grandma's favorite movie."

"It's my favorite too!" said Mrs. Mason.

If Brooke were honest, she loved it as well. She'd watched it at her grandma's house a hundred times.

"I've never heard of it," Eva said. "Why is the tour in Salzburg?"

"Because the story takes place in Salzburg," Mrs. Mason said.

"Why don't we know about this movie in Austria?" Eva asked.

Herr Mueller answered, "It's famous in the United States, but it was never famous here."

"Why not?" Eva asked.

"Because." Herr Mueller seemed to struggle for words. "Because the movie takes place during a hard time for Austria. We don't always like to remember what it was like then."

"You mean like when the story of the other Eva Mueller happened?"

Brooke was impressed that Eva made that connection so quickly.

Herr Mueller looked at her and nodded. "Something like that, *Liebling.*"

Brooke loved the *Sound of Music* tour. No. She loved, loved, loved it. They saw the places where all the famous parts of the movie had been filmed. Mrs. Mason sang every song that went with each scene. Brooke could have been MORTIFIED. (Eva didn't know the meaning of that word, so Brooke had to explain that it meant EMBARRASSED to DEATH.) She wasn't, though, because her mom had such a cool voice.

Towards the end of the tour, they stopped at a café with a broad view of a lake nestled in green

Salzburg!

hills. The café had the best *Sacher Torte* in the world. It was a to-die-for chocolate cake. Even better, it had a thin layer of apricot jam in the middle. Yummers! Of course, Brooke had never had *Sacher Torte* before. But she still knew this had to be the best in the world.

They ended the day with dinner at a sidewalk café and then dashed to the ballet. Cowgirl that she was, Brooke would have rather watched the Lipizzaner horses perform. She knew Austria was famous for them. But she had to admit the ballet was all right.

Eva, of course, thought she'd died and gone to heaven.

In fact, the whole day couldn't have been more spectacular. That is, until they drove onto the hedge-lined lane of Schloss Mueller and saw the light in the attic. It was exactly where the secret room was.

Chapter Ten

A Midnight Trip to the Attic

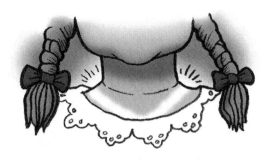

"No. I'm not going up to the secret room tonight," Brooke insisted. The girls were in their pajamas and ready for bed.

"You're, you're a . . . what's the American word?" Eva asked.

"A chicken." Brooke sighed. "But I'm not one. I just have more common sense than you."

"Oh really." Eva huffed, stuck out her lower lip, and stared at her.

"Yes. Really." Brooke couldn't believe they were having this conversation. She was NOT going to go into the attic. At night. In the dark.

"Well, then you're a chicken."

"I am NOT."

"Then why won't you go with me?"

"Because what if Drew is still in the attic? What if . . . what if he found the locket, and we surprised him? What would he do?"

"Brooke, what's the worst that could happen?"

"Oh, no. You're not getting me with that question again."

"Okay. You be a chicken." Eva paused. "Now why do Americans call people who are scared a chicken?"

"I don't know." Brooke was annoyed. How was she supposed to know why people who weren't brave were called chickens? "All I know is that it's dumb to go in the attic in the middle of the night without a flashlight."

"It's not the middle of the night. It's only 11:00."

Eva rolled her eyes. "Besides, I have a flashlight." She pulled a small flashlight out of a drawer and grinned. "Are you coming?"

What could Brooke say? "Okay." She groaned. "But if I die, it'll be your fault."

Eva laughed. Clearly, she didn't understand.

The two girls quietly opened the bedroom door and crept into the hall.

Voices drifted up from the kitchen. They heard Herr Mueller laugh. The hall was dark and quiet though.

That was a good thing.

Eva opened the attic door. It squeaked.

They held their breaths. Nothing changed. The kitchen door didn't open. The voices didn't grow louder.

Both of them breathed again.

Quietly, they took each step. The third one creaked. So did the seventh one. With every noise, they paused.

"They can't hear us up here," Eva whispered.

Brooke nodded. She was holding her breath. In

a few more minutes, she would pass out from lack of oxygen.

Finally, they reached the wardrobe. Once again, Eva climbed in first. Brooke just shook her head and followed. If her mother caught her, she'd be on the next plane home. So much for the wonders of an "international friendship."

Eva's flashlight shone high and low. The boxes covered in sheets looked the same. The secret room looked the same. The table and chairs, the tea set, the doll—everything looked in place. That is, until they checked the doll's neck.

Sure enough, the locket was gone!

Chapter Eleven

Eva Mueller

"That thief!" Brooke shouted and pounded the table with her fist.

"We're going to get him. Come on!"

The two girls clattered down the stairs and into the kitchen. Frau Eder stood at the stove and fussed with a pan of fresh *Kaiserschmarrn*. Herr Mueller, Mrs. Mason, and Drew sat at the table. All of them had mugs of steaming coffee.

"There you are!" Eva said and pointed to Drew.

"Ah, Liebling." Herr Mueller reached out to his granddaughter. "I knew we wouldn't be able to keep the *Kaiserschmarrn* a secret."

"Grandfather, call the police. That man is a thief!" Eva said and pointed again at the young man.

"I haven't stolen anything," Drew said and stood up. His hands clenched into fists at his sides.

"Don't lie to us," Brooke said. "The locket is missing, and you're the only one who could have taken it."

"I didn't steal the locket." Drew narrowed his eyes. His voice had a hard edge to it.

"I don't believe you. If you're dishonest enough to steal a locket, you wouldn't have any trouble lying about it."

"I tell you I didn't take it." He rubbed his neck and looked at the adults in the room.

"No? Then where is it?" Eva asked. "It's not where we hid it. And you had the whole day to look for it while we were in Salzburg."

"Look. I'll be honest with you. I did go look for it, but not for the reasons you think."

"What's that supposed to mean?" Brooke asked.

"It means," Herr Mueller interrupted. His voice sounded strangely soft. "That he doesn't have the locket."

"You believe him?" Eva sounded outraged.

"Yes, I do." Herr Mueller put his hand into his pocket and pulled out the locket. He set it on the table.

"You? Grandfather! Why?"

"It's complicated."

"I know. And it's long and sad and you think I'm too young." Eva's lips tightened and she crossed her arms.

"Herr Mueller," Brooke began. Her voice shook. She didn't know if she had enough nerve to say what she wanted to say. "I don't want to be rude, but I think you need to tell Eva about the other Eva Mueller. Sometimes *not* knowing something is worse than knowing the truth. Imaginations can be dangerous."

Mrs. Mason reached over and gently pulled Brooke on to her lap. She wrapped her arms around her and gave her a quick kiss on the cheek. Brooke felt much, much better. No matter what Herr Mueller said or did, she'd said the right thing.

"That's a pretty wise—and brave—thing for such a small girl to say, Brooke." He stared at his coffee cup and sighed. "I guess I owe you all the story. Drew, you're welcome to listen too. I don't know what you were doing poking around my house while we were gone. But I suspect you also have a story to tell us."

Frau Eder put the pan of *Kaiserschmarrn* and a dish of applesauce on the table along with forks and plates for everyone. They all helped themselves while Herr Mueller began to talk.

"It all happened back in the 1930s. Things weren't good here in Europe. We had a depression just like you did in the United States. People didn't have jobs or money. We were lucky to live in this area and own land because we knew we would at least be able to eat. We lost a lot of our wealth during that time. But that's not the sad part. You can always make money again."

He took a sip of coffee and continued.

"It was especially bad because Hitler came to power in Germany. Now Germany and Austria share a lot of things. We have the same language, a lot of the same foods, and even a long border. We even shared Hitler in a way because he was born in Austria and ruled Germany. Our countries are like two cousins. There were plenty of people in Austria who liked Hitler and plenty who didn't. Even within families people disagreed. Our family included, Eva." He looked sad as he said this.

"My father had a brother named Klaus. Now Klaus argued with his father all the time about Hitler. Klaus didn't like Hitler and was afraid of what he was going to do to Austria and the rest of Europe. But my grandfather thought Hitler would bring prosperity again. My father, whose name was Andreas, agreed more with his brother Klaus. But he didn't want to make their father mad, so most of the time he didn't get into the arguments."

"But what does this have to do with Eva, Grandfather?"

"I'm getting to that, *Liebling*. There are just so many things you need to understand before I tell you about her." He tousled her hair. "Finally, the arguments got so bad that Klaus said he was leaving. He meant not just Schloss Mueller but Austria, too. My grandfather was so angry that he told him to leave that very moment and never return."

Herr Mueller shook his head. "I can't ever imagine sending my child away like that. It was a terrible, terrible thing. People think the war was the worst thing that ever happened to Austria. But before the first shot was even fired, the war destroyed our family."

"And where does the other Eva come in?" Eva put her arm on her grandfather's shoulder as if to comfort him.

"Eva was Klaus's little girl. She was quite a bit older than me. I think she might have been nine at the time." He smiled at the two girls. "Just the age that you are, so you were right about that. Anyway, Klaus's wife died soon after Eva was born. That would have been an even worse thing except that my parents had just gotten married. My mother loved little Eva with all her heart. She treated her like the daughter she always wanted."

He opened the locket and looked at the two pictures. "When Klaus left, he of course took Eva with him. My mother was away for the day. When she returned, Eva was gone. She never even got to say goodbye."

"But they came back after the war, didn't they? I mean the whole family was together again later, right?" Eva asked. There was a lot of hope in her voice.

Herr Mueller shook his had. "That's one of the

very sad parts of the story. We don't know what happened to Klaus and Eva. The family never heard from them again."

"How awful!" Brooke felt her mom's arms tighten around her. She sniffed back her tears.

"My father says my mother was never quite the same after that. When I was born, she loved me with all her heart, except for the small part of her heart where she always carried Eva."

Eva—the one who was flesh and blood and standing in the kitchen—grabbed a tissue. She wiped her eyes and blew her nose.

Herr Mueller fingered the locket again. "Mother told me Eva had a secret playroom—that's how Eva had talked about it. When Klaus and Eva left, my mother made my father close up the playroom with everything just as it was. He must have moved the wardrobe in front of the door. "

He squeezed his granddaughter. "So, you see,

I knew about the playroom, but I never knew exactly where it was. When you came running into the room to tell me you'd found a secret room on the other side of the wardrobe, I should have been happy for you to find it. Instead, my only thoughts were about how the room made my mother sad."

"So when did you go look for the locket?"

"The funny thing is I didn't even know there was a locket. I went up there last night after you girls were in bed. I wanted to see this room for myself. When I lifted the doll, I realized there was a locket under her dress. I didn't know you knew about it, too, or I wouldn't have taken it."

He rubbed the shiny silver one more time and then handed it to Eva. "This should be yours to keep. The pictures of those two people are very special to us even though they've been gone a long time. The photos are of my mother and Eva."

Eva put the locket on. She took a deep breath.

"I'll wear it forever and ever."

"My mother," Herr Mueller continued, "was very old when you were born. When your parents named you Eva, it made her so happy. It was like that part of her heart could finally heal. She died a few months later, but she was at peace in a way she'd never been before."

The little crowd in the kitchen was silent for a few minutes. And then Brooke remembered why they'd come downstairs so late at night in the first place. "But that doesn't tell us why you," she pointed at the young man at the table, "went to steal the locket."

Drew's eyes were watery. He rested his elbows on the table and folded his hands. He laid his forehead on his hands. His shoulders rose up and down with each deep breath. Finally, he looked up. "Is it stealing if you take something back that already belongs to you?"

"What do you mean? How could you possibly think that locket is yours?" Eva said. She wrapped her hand around the silver heart.

Drew looked her in the eye. "Because it belongs to my grandmother."

"Your grandmother? You mean—"

He nodded. "My grandmother is Eva Mueller." He laughed for the first time that evening. "The *first* Eva Mueller."

"You mean she's alive?" Herr Mueller said softly. It was as though he didn't dare believe what he'd just heard.

"Alive and doing well for someone who is almost 90." He smiled broadly.

"So that's how you recognized the *Edelweiss* pattern on the cover," Brooke said. It all made sense now. What had he said when he traced the letter? It was specially made for a special little girl. "You knew to look for the locket."

Eva Mueller

Drew nodded. "My grandmother told me lots of stories about Schloss Mueller." He looked at Herr Mueller. "I know it's too late, but my grandmother missed your mother every bit as much as your mother missed her." He smiled at Eva. "You know, you weren't the only one named for a relative. My full name is Andrew—"

"For Andreas," Herr Mueller finished the sentence. "You were named for my father."

Drew smiled. "She told me to always be proud of that name. He was the peacemaker in the family. Grandmother has told me every single thing she can remember about those years, even the secret playroom and the locket."

"That's why you came looking for work here," Herr Mueller said. "But why didn't you tell us who you were?"

Drew sighed. "I should have, but I honestly didn't know how you would treat me. My great-grandfather, Klaus Mueller, had filled my grandmother with awful stories about how the family would be treated if any of us ever returned. She never believed it, though. She only remembered all the love she felt as a child, even from her grandfather, the man who sent Klaus away."

"This calls for a family reunion!" Herr Mueller said. "Is she well enough to travel?"

"She's well enough to do lots of things, including get on a plane."

"Then get on the phone." Herr Mueller handed the phone to Drew. "Call her. It's only late afternoon in Wyoming. It's time she comes back home."

"And tell her that when she comes," Eva said and took off the locket, "I have a gift for her."

Mystery at the Christmas Market

Chapter One

"Do you see them yet, Brooke?" Eva asked. She felt a tiny bit out of breath from running up the stairs and crawling through the wardrobe to get into their secret room in the attic.

"No. Just that black car out on the road." Brooke's nose nearly touched the frosty window.

"It's still there?"

Brooke nodded. "Did you get the binoculars?"

"Yes. But I had to sneak them out of the library. Frau Eder was dusting in the dining room. She wouldn't be happy if she knew I brought them up here." Eva unbuckled the leather case. She carefully lifted out the antique binoculars.

Brooke picked up the binoculars and held them up to her eyes. They weighed a ton compared to the

91

ones her dad had back in Colorado.

"What are they doing?" Eva asked.

"I can't tell."

"But why are they just sitting there by the road?"

Brooke shrugged her shoulders. "Who knows?"

"Let me see."

Eva touched Brooke's arm. "Wait a minute, Brooke. People are getting out of the car."

Even without the binoculars, Brooke could see two people step out of the car onto the snow-packed road.

"Let me see!"

Eva handed the binoculars to Brooke, who put them up to her eyes. "It's a man and a woman," Brooke said. "The man has bright red hair. Crazy red. I can see that from here. The woman is wearing a red scarf around her neck."

Brooke watched the woman walk around to the driver's side and join the man. They both stared up at the castle, or *Schloss*.

"She's pointing up at Schloss Mueller." Brooke tried to focus her eyes better. "Uh oh. They have binoculars too. And they're looking up at us."

The girls scooted back from the window.

"Do you think they saw us?" Eva asked. Her heart pounded, but she didn't quite know why. After all, Brooke and she were in Schloss Mueller where they were supposed to be. The strangers were the ones doing something suspicious.

Find out what happens to Brooke and Eva in the Pack-n-Go Girls book, Mystery at the Christmas Market.

Meet More Pack-n-Go Girls!

Discover Australia with Wendy and Chloe!

Mystery of the Min Min Lights

It's hot. It's windy. It's dusty. It's the Australian outback. Wendy Lee arrives from California. She's lucky to meet Chloe Taylor, who invites Wendy to their sheep station. It sounds like fun except that someone is stealing the sheep. And the thief just might be something as crazy as a UFO.

Discover Brazil with Sofia and Júlia!

Mystery of the Troubled Toucan

Nine-year-old Sofia Diaz's world is coming apart. So is the rickety old boat that carries her far up the Rio Negro river in Brazil. Crocodiles swim in the dark waters. Spiders scurry up the twisted tree trunks. And a crazy toucan screeches a warning. It chases Sofia and Júlia, her new friend, deep into the steamy rainforest. There they stumble upon a shocking discovery. Don't miss the second Brazil book, *Mystery of the Lazy Loggerhead.*

Meet More Pack-n-Go Girls!

Discover Mexico with Izzy and Patti!

Mystery of the Thief in the Night

Izzy's family sails into a quiet lagoon in Mexico and drops their anchor. Izzy can't wait to explore the pretty little village, eat yummy tacos, and practice her Spanish. When she meets nine-year-old Patti, Izzy's thrilled. Now she can do all that and have a new friend to play with too. Life is perfect. At least it's perfect until they realize there's a midnight thief on the loose! Don't miss the second Mexico book, *Mystery of the Disappearing Dolphin.*

Discover Thailand with Jess and Nong May!

Mystery of the Golden Temple

Nong May and her family have had a lot of bad luck lately. When nine-year-old Jess arrives in Thailand and accidentally breaks a special family treasure, it seems to only get worse. It turns out the treasure holds a secret that could change things forever!

What to Know Before You Go!

Where is Austria?

Schoolchildren in Austria learn their country is shaped like
a shoe. Can you see why they think that? Austria is in the
southeastern area of Europe. It is completely surrounded by
land. Austria has eight other countries as neighbors: Czech
Republic, Germany, Hungary, Italy, Liechtenstein, Slovakia,
Slovenia, and Switzerland. It's not a very big country. It's about
the size of Maine. But it's a beautiful country full of forests
and mountains. Because it has so many mountains, it's well
known for its great skiing.

How Big is Austria?

Austria is about the same size as the state of Maine in the United States. Austria has many more people, though. As of 2010, Austria has 8,384,745 people. Maine has only 1,328,302 people. So even though they are the same size, Austria has over 7,000,000 more people than Maine. Almost half of Maine's population lives in or close to Portland, Maine. If you drive through Maine, you'll travel through lots of the state where no people live. In Austria, you'll see lots of small towns and farms everywhere.

Austrian Money

Did you know that every country has its own money? In the United States, we use dollars and cents for our money system. Austrians use euros and cents. This is the currency, or money, for all of the European Union. We use this symbol to mean dollar: $. This is the symbol for the euro: €. In the U.S., we use a period (.) between dollars and cents. Europeans use a comma (,). If Brooke buys ice cream in Colorado, the price looks like this: $2.75. When Brooke and Eva buy ice cream in Austria, the price looks like this: €2,75.

Cities in Austria

If you go to Austria, be sure to visit both Vienna and Salzburg. Vienna is the capital of the country. The Austrian name for Vienna is Wien, pronounced Veen. Over a million and a half people live in Vienna and the surrounding area. Be sure to visit the Hofburg or Schönbrunn palaces. Both are stunning. Plan to attend a concert or an opera in the historic city center, too. It's fun to listen to music that was composed in Vienna 200 years ago by Franz Schubert and Johann Strauss, who were born there.

Salzburg is less than a tenth the size of Vienna, but its beauty and history are just as amazing. Wolfgang Amadeus Mozart was born in Salzburg. Many other musicians of his era played there. As a result, you can always find a concert or opera to go to. The city center of Salzburg survived World War II and so the cathedrals, palaces, and government buildings are much like they were hundreds of years ago. With the Salzach River winding through the city, twisting cobblestone streets, and endless window boxes overflowing with flowers, every photo you'll take will be pretty as a post card.

What Austrians Eat

You won't have trouble finding familiar foods in Austria. Traditionally, though, Austrians eat meat and vegetables that are fried in a pan. A favorite dish is *Wiener Schnitzel*, which is a thin slice of veal coated in breadcrumbs and fried.

Recipe for Wiener Schnitzel

Ingredients *(If you make this recipe, be sure to get an adult to help you.):*

- 1 ½ pounds of thin veal cutlets (You can also use boneless beef, pork, or chicken.)
- ½ cup flour
- 3 T. grated Parmesan cheese

- 1 t. minced parsley
- ½ t. salt
- ¼ t. pepper
- 2 eggs
- 2 T. water

- 1 cup dry breadcrumbs
- 6 T. oil or lard (lard is traditional)
- 1 lemon sliced into quarters
- Cranberry sauce

1. Place each veal cutlet between two pieces of wax paper and pound with a meat mallet until about ¼" thick.

2. Mix the flour, Parmesan cheese, parsley, salt, and pepper together. Dredge cutlets in the flour mixture until the surface is completely dry.

3. Mix the water and eggs together. Dip the meat in the egg mixture and then roll quickly in the breadcrumbs until coated. Don't press the breadcrumbs into the meat.

4. Heat the oil for frying to 350 degrees. You should have about ¼" of oil in the pan. This will keep the meat from sticking to the pan. Also, the breading will take on less oil than if it's sticking to the pan. Fry the schnitzel on each side for 3 to 4 minutes. Remove the schnitzel from the pan and briefly place on a paper towel to absorb excess oil.

5. Serve with the lemon wedges to squeeze over the schnitzel. Pass a bowl of cranberry sauce, which is also a traditional topping for schnitzel.

Say It in German!

Grüß Gott!

English	German	German Pronunciation
Hello	Hallo	Hahl-lō
Hello (Good day)	Grüß Gott	Grōss gŏt
Good day	Guten Tag	Gū-tĕn tahg
Good morning	Guten Morgen	Gū-tĕn morgen
Good night	Guten Abend	Gū-tĕn ah-bend
Hi	Hi/Tag	Tahg
Goodbye	Auf Wiedersehen	Auf vē-der-zähn
Bye	Tschuess	Tchoos
Please	Bitte	Bĭ-tah
Thank you (very much)	Danke (schön)/ (Vielen Dank)	Dahn-kah (feel-en dahnk)
Excuse me	Entschuldigen Sie mich	Ĕnt-shū-lĭ-gĕn zee mĭck
Yes/No	Ja/Nein	Yah/Nine
Enjoy the meal	Guten Appetit	Gū-tĕn a-pĕ-teet
Grandfather	Grossvater	Grōss vahter
Mrs./Miss	Frau/Fräulein	Frow/Frow-line
Mr.	Herr	Hair
Castle	Schloss	Shlōss
Sweetheart	Liebling	Leeb-lĭng

English	German	German Pronunciation
When?	Wann?	Vahn
Why?	Warum?	Var-ūm
What?	Was?	Vahs
Who?	Wer?	Vair
Where?	Wo?	Vo
How?	Wie?	Vee
How much/many?	Wieviel/Wie viele?	Vee-fel/vee fēlah
Is/are there?	Gibt es?	Gĭbt ĕs
What is it?	Was ist das?	Vahs ist dahs
0	Null	Null
1	Eins	Īnz
2	Zwei	Zvī
3	Drei	Drī
4	Vier	Fear
5	Fünf	Funf
6	Sechs	Zĕchs
7	Sieben	Zēbĕn
8	Acht	Ahcht
9	Neun	Noin
10	Zehn	Zāne

Do you speak German? If so, you might notice *Herr* Mueller is used in some places where the correct German form is *Herrn* Mueller. So English readers aren't confused, Herr Mueller is used throughout as the character's name.

My Austrian Trip Planner

Where to go: _____

_____

_____

_____

_____

_____

_____

_____

_____

_____

_____

_____

_____

_____

_____

_____

My Austrian Trip Planner

What to do:

My Austrian Trip Planner

Things I want to pack:

_____

_____

_____

_____

_____

_____

_____

_____

_____

_____

_____

_____

_____

_____

Friends to send postcards to:

My Austrian Trip Planner

_____

_____

_____

_____

_____

_____

_____

_____

_____

_____

_____

_____

Thank you to the following Pack-n-Go Girls:

Meredith Rainhart
Skylar Stanley
Sarah Travis

Thank you also to Linda Hackman, Althea Harvey, Andrea Rieger, Jeannie Sheeks, Heather Walton, and Helene Wetzel.

And a special thanks to my Pack-n-Go Girls co-founder, Lisa Travis, and our husbands, Steve Diller and Rich Travis, who have been along with us on this adventure.

106

 **Janelle Diller** has always had a passion for writing. As a young child, she wouldn't leave home without a pad and pencil just in case her novel hit her and she had to scribble it down quickly. She eventually learned good writing takes a lot more time and effort than this. Fortunately, she still loves to write. She's especially lucky because she also loves to travel. She's explored over 45 countries for work and play and can't wait to land in the next new country. It doesn't get any better than writing stories about traveling. Janelle and her husband split their time between a sailboat in Mexico and a house in Colorado.

Adam Turner has been working as a freelance illustrator since 1987. He has illustrated coloring books, puzzle books, magazine articles, game packaging, and children's books. He's loved to draw ever since he picked up his first pencil as a toddler. Instead of doing the usual two-year-old thing of chewing on it or poking his eye out  with it, he actually put it on paper and thus began the journey. Adam also loves to travel and has had some crazy adventures. He's swum with crocodiles in the Zambezi, jumped out of a perfectly good airplane, and even fished for piranha in the Amazon. It's a good thing drawing relaxes his nerves! Adam lives in Arizona with his wife and their daughter.

Pack-n-Go Girls Online

Dying to know when the next Pack-n-Go Girls book will be out? Want to learn more German or how to yodel? Trying to figure out what to pack for your next trip? Looking for cool family travel tips? Interested in some fun learning activities about Austria to use at home or at school while you are reading *Mystery of the Secret Room*?

- Check out our website:
  www.packngogirls.com
- Follow us on Twitter:
  @packngogirls
- Like us on Facebook:
  facebook.com/packngogirls
- Follow us on Instagram:
  packngogirlsadventures
- Discover great ideas on Pinterest:
  Pack-n-Go Girls

59836212R00069

Made in the USA
San Bernardino, CA
07 December 2017